# *Tales of* Enchantment

Also by Pleasant DeSpain

THE BOOKS OF NINE LIVES

VOLUME SEVEN

# Tales of
# Enchantment

Pleasant DeSpain

Illustrations by Don Bell

August House Publishers, Inc.
LITTLE ROCK

Published 2003 by August House Publishers, Inc.
P.O. Box 3223, Little Rock, Arkansas 72203
www.augusthouse.com.

Printed in the United States of America

10   9   8   7   6   5   4   3   2   1     HB

LIBRARY OF CONGRESS CATALOGING-IN-PUBLICATION DATA

DeSpain, Pleasant.
    Tales of enchantment / by Pleasant DeSpain ; illustrations by Don Bell.
       p.   cm.   — (The books of nine lives ; v. 7)
    Includes bibliographical references.
    Contents: The book of magic : Russia—The three aunties : Norway—
Red Cap and the miser : Ireland—The shoemaker and the elves :
Germany—The seven stars : Cherokee—The old man with a wart :
Japan—The birds of all the world : Spain—The silver bell : Denmark—
The shoemaker's dream : Holland.
    ISBN 0-87483-711-1 (alk. paper)
    1. Tales. [1. Folklore.] I. Bell, Don, 1935– ill. II. Title
PZ8.1.D453 Taff 2003
[398.2]—dc21                                                                                          2003050207

Executive editor: Liz Parkhurst
Project editor: April McGee
Text designer: Liz Lester
Cover and book illustration: Don Bell

The paper used in this publication meets the minimum requirements
of the American National Standard for Information Sciences—
Permanence of Paper for Printed Library Materials, ANSI Z39.48–1984.

AUGUST HOUSE          PUBLISHERS          LITTLE ROCK

for Gary Feazell and Douglas Geier,
brothers of my heart and soul

### *Acknowledgments*

I'm fortunate to have genuine friends and colleagues without whose help the continuation of this series would not have been possible. Genuine thanks to:

- Liz and Ted Parkhurst, Publishers
- Don Bell, Illustrator
- April McGee, Project Editor
- Margaret Read MacDonald, Storyteller, Author, Librarian
- Jennifer D. Murphy, Head of the Children's Department, Albany, New York Public Library
- Candace E. Deisley, Youth Services Librarian, Albany, New York Public Library
- Deidre McGrath, Youth Services Librarian, Albany, New York Public Library
- Denver Public Library
- Lakewood, Colorado, Public Library
- Seattle Public Library
- University of Washington Library (Seattle)

# The Books of Nine Lives Series

A good story lives each time it's read and told again. The stories in this series have had many lives over the centuries. My retellings have had several lives in the past twenty-plus years, and I'm pleased to witness their new look and feel. All but two of the stories in this volume were originally published in "Pleasant Journeys," my weekly column in *The Seattle Times,* during 1977–78, and collected into a two-volume set entitled *Pleasant Journeys: Tales to Tell from Around the World,* in 1979. The books were republished as *Twenty-Two Splendid Tales to Tell From Around the World* a few years later and remained in print for twenty-one years and three editions.

Now, in 2003, the time has come for a fresh presentation of these ageless, universal, useful, and so-very-human tales.

I'm profoundly grateful to all the teachers,

parents, storytellers, and children who have found these tales worthy of sharing. One story always leads to the next. May these lead you to laughter, wisdom, and delight. As evolving human beings, we are more alike than we are different, each with a story to tell.

—*Pleasant DeSpain*
*Troy, New York*

# Contents

# Introduction

There is time for magic in the storyteller's life and work. Attributes such as transformation, sorcery, and supernatural powers lead to enchantment, something found in all stories worth telling. The magician, in this case the teller of the tale, allows the story, teller, and listener to become one. The power of magic is at work.

Some of my earliest memories as a spellbound listener were as a child at bedtime. My mother read picture books and Bible stories to my one-year-older brother and me, sending us to sleep always wanting more. A few years later I discovered intense radio dramas with realistic sound effects and spine-chilling music. "The Shadow knows . . ." became a popular refrain in ours and many other households, more than fifty years past.

One of the most valuable lessons of my

storytelling life is that time, like magic, is always fluid and never static. We, as tellers of tales, have the gift of both time and the inherent magic of story to hone our craft and practice our art.

Because magic is universal, I've included nine traditional stories from throughout the world in this multicultural collection. Here you'll discover tales from Russia, Norway, Ireland, Germany, the Cherokee Nation, Japan, Spain, Denmark, and Holland. You'll meet demons, shoemakers, men and women both young and old, boys who become stars of the night sky, leprechauns, dwarfs, and the power of dreams. Here you'll likely meet a part of yourself.

Read and share these tales. Magic never grows old. Magic always has time.

# The Book of Magic

*Russia*

Long ago, a retired soldier inherited a book on magic from his uncle, who had recently passed away. The book was thick and heavy. It smelled old and musty. He lit a candle late one night and began to read. He read aloud, sounding out the strange names listed in row after row on the brittle pages. "This is an odd book if ever I held one," he muttered to himself. "It's nothing but weird names. Whoever heard of *Joespanath?* And what in the world is a *Braggourth?* And what does *Moonslayed* mean?"

Rippaltoe
Doleafragpom
Joespanath
Dorsaldoot
Moonslayed
Rowabullo
Braggourth
TassaKloe
Zartoast

Suddenly he heard a dark laugh. Someone else was in the room, standing in the shadows. He heard another laugh, then a groan. It wasn't just one someone. There were many. Thirty demons from the underworld had come at his bidding, ten for each name spoken. Thirty demons anxious to perform dark deeds.

The soldier was petrified. He didn't know what to do and kept on reading. "*Tassakloe, Leafragpom, Dorsaldoom . . .*"

Thirty more demons arrived.

"*Rowabullo, Rippaltoe, Zartoast . . .*"

Now there were ninety crowding the room.

The soldier slammed the book shut and let it fall to the floor. "What have I done? What will I do? What will become of me?" he cried.

Growing restless, the demons chanted:

> *Give us a task, tell us now.*
> *Give us a task, tell us now.*
> *Tell us what to do!*

Thinking quickly, the man said, "Sharpen the swords of every soldier in Russia."

Without another word, the demons flew out his window and into the night. They

returned an hour later. "It's done," said one of
the foul creatures. Then all ninety chanted:

> *Give us a task, tell us now.*
> *Give us a task, tell us now.*
> *Tell us what to do!*

*I made it too easy,* thought the soldier.
Suddenly he had a brilliant idea. "Using a
small cup, give every tree in Russia a drink
from the Volga River."

The demons flew into the night. They
returned an hour later. "It's done," said
another of the evil spirits. And again, they all
chanted:

> *Give us a task, tell us now.*
> *Give us a task, tell us now.*
> *Tell us what to do!*

The man was at his wits' end. He had to

pound of flax.

return tomorrow morning," said the

locking the door behind her.

e began to cry. Never before had she

ax into yarn. Never before had she

such a fix.

denly, an old woman with an ugly,

se appeared before her. "What is

child?" she asked.

wiped her eyes and explained.

u promise to call me 'auntie' on your

day, I'll spin the flax for you," said

oman.

greed and lay down to sleep. When

e the next morning, all the flax had

n into a soft and fine yarn. The

s delighted, and that made the

aids even more envious. They told

that Rose had boasted that she

ve all the yarn into a fine cloth in a

think of something even more difficult. "Count every ant that crawls. Count every bird that flies. And . . . count every star in the sky."

Off they flew, eager to do their work. They returned two hours later. "It's done," they declared. The chanting resumed:

> *Give us a task, tell us now.*
> *Give us a task, tell us now.*
> *Tell us what to do!*

The soldier was defeated. There wasn't anything they couldn't accomplish. He sat on the floor next to the magic book. It opened to the page he had last read. "What will I do? Oh, what will I do?" he said.

The demons crowded around him, awaiting his command. They grew agitated and more threatening. "Tell us what to do!" they demanded.

*Zartoast,* the last name he had read from the book, glowed bright on the page. He said it aloud, and ten of the demons disappeared. Then he understood the book's secret. By reading the names from first to last, the demons appeared. By reading the names from last to first, they disappeared.

He quickly said, "*Rippaltoe, Rowabullo, Dorsaldoom, Leafragpom, Tassakloe, Moonslayed, Braggourth, Joespanath.* All of you be gone!"

And they were gone, all ninety demons. The soldier wiped his brow and closed the magic book. He put it in a leather sack and sewed the sack shut. He locked the sack in a strong wooden box and buried the box deep in his yard. Never again did he say those strange names aloud, neither first to last nor last to first.

# The Three Aunti

*Norway*

Once, long ago, a named Rose kn and asked for work. her and gave Rose a worked hard, but th grew jealous of her queen that Rose h; pound of flax into

"If she says sh do it," said the qu

Rose was take tle cellar. It cont

and a
"I'l
queen
Ros
spun f
been i
Sud
long no
wrong,
Rose
"If y
wedding
the old
Rose
she awol
been spu
queen wa
kitchen n
the queen
could wea
single day

The queen took Rose to another cellar room containing the yarn and a loom, and wished her God-speed. Again Rose began to cry. Suddenly, an old woman appeared. This one had an ugly hump on her back.

"Why do you cry, pretty one?" she asked.

Rose told her all about it, and the old woman said, "If you promise to call me 'auntie' on your wedding day, I'll weave the yarn for you."

The lass promised and lay down to sleep. When she awoke the next morning, she found that the yarn had been woven into a beautiful piece of linen cloth. The queen was so pleased that she called Rose her favorite servant. The kitchen maids were furious and told the queen that now Rose had boasted that she could sew the linen into six shirts in one day.

The poor girl was put into a third cellar room with a pair of scissors, a needle and thread, and the linen cloth. Once again, she began to cry. Before long, a third old woman appeared before her. This one had ugly, red eyes as large as saucers. Rose told her the reason for her tears and explained that she had never before sewn a shirt.

"If you will call me 'auntie' on your wedding day, I'll sew the shirts for you."

The young girl agreed and lay down to sleep. When she awoke the following morning, the six shirts were made. The queen thought that they were so lovely that she called to her son, the prince, and explained how skilled Rose was at spinning, weaving, and sewing. The prince was impressed with Rose's skills and charmed by her beauty. When he asked Rose to marry him, she happily agreed.

A grand party was held on the wedding day, and three of the invited guests were the old women who had helped Rose.

"Good day and welcome, my aunties three," said Rose.

"How can they be your aunts?" asked the horrified prince. "You are so beautiful, and they are so ugly."

"We were pretty when we were young," said the first old woman. "I got my long nose by sitting at the spinning wheel each day, year after year, nodding over the whirling yarn."

The second old woman said, "I got the hump on my back from bending over the loom each day, year after year."

"And I," explained the third woman, "got my red eyes by staring at the tiny stitches as I sewed each day, year after year."

After thinking for a long moment, the prince declared, "From this day forth, my beautiful bride shall neither spin nor weave nor sew."

Rose smiled at her three aunties, just as they smiled in return.

# Red Cap and the Miser

*Ireland*

Once there was a stingy old man named Phillip. He was so stingy that his neighbors often said he had sold his hair to the leprechauns for pillow stuffing. That was why his head was as bald as a hard-boiled egg.

It wasn't like Phillip to give anything away, and when he discovered that a bit of fresh milk was missing from the big milk can in the barn, he was furious. "I'll catch the thief, and he will pay double—no, triple—for what he took! You just wait and see, Annie."

Annie was his wife, and she had listened to his ranting for many a long year. "Ah, to be sure, it's but a wee bit that's gone. We'll not miss it."

"Nobody takes my milk without paying for it," declared Phillip. "I'll hide in the barn tonight and catch me a thief, that I will."

Hiding behind a large pile of hay, the farmer watched Red Cap, the leprechaun, walk up to the milk can with a tiny pail in hand. Phillip jumped out in front of him, startling the wee fellow, and said with an angry sneer, "I've caught you red-handed, you little sneak. What do you say to that?"

"I say that you're an old miser and a grouch, Phillip. You're always complaining that my thorn tree grows too close to your cornfield. Now you accuse me of stealing your milk. Your father always gave me a bit, and your grandfather did as well. But you must be paid. And how much is it that I owe?"

"I want gold for all the milk you've taken from me and from my father and his father too. I also want payment for all the years you've lived under the thorn tree. If you don't give me enough gold to cover your debt, I'll cut the tree down and grow corn in its place."

Suddenly, the leprechaun yanked his red cap from his head and tossed it high into the air. *Plop!* It landed on Phillip's bald head, and there it stayed. He pulled and tugged and jerked, but it wouldn't budge an inch.

"You want payment, do you?" asked Red Cap. "You want to cut down my thorn tree, do you? You want to grow corn in its place, do you? Well, I'll give you corn, I will!" So saying, he skipped out the barn door in the wink of an eye.

Phillip went back into the house wearing the red cap. His wife pulled with all her strength, but still it wouldn't come off. He had to wear it to bed. When he awoke in the morning, he felt something growing under the cap. "It's hair, Annie! That thieving leprechaun has given me hair."

Annie used her scissors to split a seam and look inside the cap. "If it's hair, then it's green with little ears growing on stalks. It's corn that you're growing, husband, not hair."

"I'm bewitched!" cried Phillip. "That old leprechaun has won. Get me six eggs and a pound of sweet butter, Annie. I'll go apologize."

Phillip walked to the thorn tree and called, "Red Cap, please take these gifts. You can have all the milk you want from now on. Just take the cap from my head, please."

"Will you put a nice fence around my tree, and bring me a bit of cheese each week?" asked the leprechaun from under the tree. He missed his cap, and besides, he had played his joke.

"Yes," said Phillip. "Whatever you want."

"Agreed," said the leprechaun, and the cap
flew from the man's head. He felt his scalp.
It was bald. Greatly relieved, Phillip walked
home. From that time forth, he remained a
stingy old man—to all but Red Cap.

# The Shoemaker and the Elves

*Germany*

There was once a poor shoemaker who had nothing left but enough supplies to make one pair of shoes. That night he cut the leather into proper-sized pieces and left them on his workbench, all ready to be sewn together.

Early the next morning, to his great amazement, he found the shoes already made. And what beautiful shoes they were! Each stitch was the work of a master craftsman. Just then a customer entered the shop and tried on the shoes. They fit him perfectly, and he happily paid a good price for them.

Now the shoemaker had enough money to buy leather for two pairs of shoes. He cut them out that night and left them on his workbench, ready to be sewn in the morning. When he awoke, he found them beautifully finished, just as before. Two customers entered the shop and gave him the funds for four pairs of shoes. He cut them out as before and left them on the workbench. The next morning the shoes were again perfectly made and ready to be sold.

Several customers were waiting at his door because news of the wonderful shoes had spread throughout the town. Each tried to outbid the other in order to buy a pair. The shoemaker made enough money to buy leather for twenty pairs of shoes and spent the rest of the day cutting them out. In the morning, twenty pairs of shoes, all stitched together and looking fine, sat on his workbench. A large crowd of townsfolk waited at his door, coins in hand.

And so it went. He cut the leather out each night, and the shoes were ready to be sold each morning. Soon he was a rich man.

One night during the month of December, the shoemaker said to his wife, "Let's stay awake tonight and see who comes to help us."

They left a candle burning on the workbench and hid behind the clothes hanging in a corner closet. As the clock struck midnight, the door to the shop opened as if by magic. Two tiny men, naked as the day they were born, ran into the room. The shoemaker's mouth dropped open as he and his wife watched the elves climb up to the workbench and set to work. They hammered and stitched so rapidly that the work was done in a few moments. They climbed down from the bench and ran out of the shop and into the cold night.

The following morning, the shoemaker's wife said, "Husband, those nice little men have made our fortune, and now it's time for us to do something for them. It's the dead of winter, and the road is covered with ice. They don't have a stitch of clothing, poor souls. I'll make them each a shirt, coat, vest, and a nice pair of trousers."

"I'll make shoes to fit their tiny feet," said the shoemaker.

On the night when everything was ready, they placed the gifts on the workbench and again hid in the closet.

The clock struck twelve and the door opened. In ran the two naked elves. They quickly climbed up to the bench, ready to hammer and sew. Instead of leather pieces, they saw the fine attire. It was just their size. The elves got dressed and began to dance and sing:

*How dandy we look*
*in our coats and our vests!*
*No more will we work*
*for now we can rest!*

They danced out the door and never came back; but from that time forth, the shoemaker had a thriving business.

# The Seven Stars

*Cherokee*

Long ago, when the world was young and the first forests were still growing, seven boys played a game called Wheel-and-Spear.

Six of the boys stood behind a line drawn in the soft dirt and held their wooden spears high. The seventh lad, whose name was Little Elk, rolled a small wheel made of stone across the grassy plain. The boys threw their spears at the wheel as it quickly rolled away from them. When it stopped, the one whose spear struck closest to it was the winner.

"Ahh," cried Little Elk. "Red Fox wins! He

has the highest score. Ready to try again?"

"Yes," said Red Fox.

The boys ran back to the throwing line, but before they could lift their spears, a loud voice came from one of the nearby lodges. "Red Fox! Stop playing your games. Come to the lodge now and eat your evening meal."

It was his mother. She was angry because Red Fox had played at the game each day for weeks.

Soon Little Elk's mother came from her lodge. She grabbed her son by the arm. "You didn't catch any fish from the river," she said angrily. "You played at your game all afternoon and we don't have trout to eat."

The other boys' mothers called them in too, and each was scolded for playing more than helping. The next day the mothers met to grind corn and talk over their problems.

"The boys spend too much time with their game," said Little Elk's mother. "My son has become lazy and neglects his duties. We must do something."

"You speak true," said Red Fox's mother. "My boy cares for nothing but the Wheel-and-Spear game. He's becoming a stranger to me. He boasts of his skill at the game and talks of nothing else. We must end this foolishness."

The other mothers agreed, and they decided on a plan. Late that night while the boys slept, the mothers took their sons' stone wheels down to the river and dropped them into the deepest pool.

The following day, after discovering their mothers' betrayal, the boys decided to run away. "Let's go to the field to dance, and never again will we return," said Little Elk.

"Yes," said Red Fox, "our mothers will not spoil our games."

The other boys agreed, and they ran to the field and formed a circle. Like swift-running deer they danced and chanted:

*We will go far, we will go far.*
*No more to return, no more to return.*

Around and around they sped. Instead of growing tired, they grew stronger. Faster they danced, and faster still, and soon their feet were no longer touching the earth.

The sun began to fall in the sky. Darkness rose. The mothers came to the field in search of their dancing sons.

"Look!" cried Little Elk's mother. "They are rising into the air."

"Quickly," yelled the mother of Red Fox. "Grab their feet and pull them down!"

The women rushed toward their sons, but the boys were rising higher and higher. The mothers leapt high, grabbing for the boys' flying feet, but couldn't reach them.

The dancing boys continued to rise until they reached the night sky. Their mothers cried out and begged them to return, but it

was of no use. The boys had turned into
seven bright stars.

If you look up at the heavens on a clear
night, you can see them dancing still.

# The Old Man with a Wart

*Japan*

Once there was an old man who had a large wart on the right side of his face. It was so large that it looked like a ripe peach growing on his cheek. It made him look funny, but he didn't complain.

One day, while up in the high mountains, the old man got caught in a terrible storm. The wind howled and the trees groaned. Lightning flashed across the sky, and a torrent of rain began to fall. He found a hollow tree and climbed inside. Here was a cozy shelter in which to wait for the storm to end.

Soon, however, he heard the voices of strangers coming toward him. They were happy voices, full of laughter and song, but they also sounded like the shrill winds and the swaying of trees in the storm.

When the strangers arrived near the tree in which the man hid, they began to build a large bonfire. In the flames' flickering light, he saw that his companions were giants with great wings folded on their backs. They were the Storm Spirits!

The old man, shivering in fear and cold, sneezed loudly. The Storm Spirits heard him and dragged him from the tree.

"Dance!" they demanded with windy voices. "Dance around the fire as we sing in the rain."

The old man loved to dance. He began to turn round and round, bending like a flower in the storm and leaping high like a deer in flight. Soon the song of the spirits grew soft, and the man began to sway like an old pine tree in a gentle breeze. When the song ended, the man sat on the wet ground to rest. The rain turned to mist, and the sun peeked through the clouds.

"Wonderful!" cried the Storm Spirits. "You must come tomorrow and dance for us again. To make certain that you'll come, we'll take this beautiful peach that grows on your face. But do not worry. We'll give it back tomorrow."

They removed his wart and let him walk down the mountainside, back to his home. When he arrived in the village, the people asked what had happened to his wart. The old man told them the story.

One of his neighbors, a man of nearly the same age, also had a large wart growing on his face. His was on his left cheek. The neighbor decided to pay a visit to the Storm Spirits the next day and have them remove his ugly wart. He climbed the mountain early in the morning and hid in the same hollow tree.

It wasn't long before the storm hit, and it was fierce! Lightning tore holes in the sky, and rain fell like fury. The old neighbor grew afraid. The Storm Spirits arrived and built their bonfire. They found the man in the tree and dragged him out.

"Dance!" they demanded. "Dance for us like you did yesterday."

He was too scared to dance. He merely stood before the Storm Spirits and trembled like a frightened rabbit. The Spirits became angry and said, "If you won't dance for us then leave us alone. Take your peach and go home."

So saying, they put the first man's wart on the right side of his neighbor's face. Then they forced the old neighbor to run down the mountainside, where he had to live out his remaining years with both large warts on his cheeks instead of just one.

# The Birds of All the World

*Spain*

Long ago, there lived a farmer who loved his daughter, Rosita, more than anything else in the world. His wife had passed on, and father and daughter lived alone in a small, rundown farmhouse. One day, the farmer found a white rose growing beside his field. He plucked it and took it home to Rosita.

"It's the most beautiful rose I've ever seen, Papa," she said happily. "I'll put it in a bowl of water."

The moment that the green stem touched the water, a high-pitched, liquid voice came from the flower. "Find me. Look among the cliffs. Look among the rocks."

"Who are you?" asked the astonished girl.

The face of a young man appeared in the water. He was the most handsome youth she had ever seen. "Please find me," he said again. "Look among the cliffs and rocks." Then he disappeared.

She left in search of the youth early the next morning. Walking throughout the fields and forest, she stopped at every large rock and cliff. Early that evening Rosita came upon a single white rose growing from a rocky cliffside. "Are you here?" she asked. "Is this where you hide?"

The flower didn't answer. A soft wind blew, and the gurgling of a nearby river caressed her ears. "Of course," she said. "He needs water."

Rosita plucked the rose and ran to the brook. Floating the flower in a quiet pool, she again saw his beautiful reflection and heard his watery voice. "You've found me. I'm under a magical spell, and only you can help me."

"What can I do?" asked Rosita. "I'm an ordinary girl. I can't undo magic."

"Go to the large estate on the other side of the forest. The mistress of the house seeks a new maid. Ask her for work."

The girl slept in the forest that night and walked to the estate early the next morning. Large fields and sturdy barns surrounded the main house. This was a wealthy estate indeed. Rosita knocked on the heavy oaken door and was surprised to find an old, tired, and crying woman on the other side.

"Come in, dear girl, come in," she said between sobs.

"Why do you cry?" Rosita asked.

"My son has been cursed by a jealous witch and now he's gone. I don't know where he is. All my servants have fled in fear of the witch, and I'm all alone."

"I'll work for you, madam."

The mistress, dabbing at her leaking eyes with a lace handkerchief, managed a smile. "How kind of you, dear girl, but first you must pass a test. The washing needs to be done. Follow me to the back of the house."

A small mountain of dirty laundry covered the floor of one room.

"Have it clean by tonight, and you can be my maid."

Rosita carried the dirty clothes down to the riverbank and wept. It was impossible to accomplish so much in a single day.

Suddenly, a large flock of birds flew overhead. There were so many birds that they blocked much of the sunlight. There were large birds, medium-sized birds, and small ones. There were red birds and black ones, as well as blue, green, yellow, white, and brown ones. The birds of all the world were represented in this marvelous flock, and they came to help. The birds picked up the garments with their beaks and claws and washed them in the flowing river water. Then they stretched the wet clothes over sun-warmed rocks to dry. When the task was accomplished, they flew away.

Rosita returned with the enormous pile of clean laundry, and the mistress rejoiced. "You will be my maid and my friend," she declared. "And as my friend, you must help me find a cure for my leaking eyes. I've been crying since the day my son was enchanted, and I can't stop. Please help me."

Rosita returned to the riverbank the next morning. While she sipped cold river water from a cup, a strange thing happened. The flock of the birds of all the world returned, and each shed a single tear into her cup. Then they flew away.

Rosita ran back to the estate, being careful to not spill a single drop. She bathed the eyes of the mistress with the precious tears, and the old woman stopped crying. She hugged Rosita tight and said, "If only you could break the spell that has captured my son."

Rosita returned to the riverbank and found another white rose growing from the cliffside. She plucked it and set it afloat. The young man's face appeared on the water's surface, smiling at her. "You've done well, but the most difficult task is at hand. The key that unlocks my spell is found on top of the mountain that looms highest in the west. It's a secret word carved into a flat rock hidden under a falcon's nest. Say the word three times, and I'll be set free."

The flock of birds of all the world arrived as if on command. Swirling around her, each loosened a feather and let it float to her feet. She gathered the feathers. Holding them in

her hand, Rosita said, "I wish to fly to the
tallest mountain in the west."

Off she flew, along with the many-sized
and multi-colored flock, all the way to the
mountaintop. The stone was under the falcon's nest. The magic word was *Washweepfly*.

Rosita understood. The word contained her three tasks.

She flew with the flock back to the riverbank. *"Washweepfly, washweepfly, washweepfly,"* she said aloud. The rock face opened as if it were a door made of stone, and out stepped the handsome young man. He took Rosita by the hand, and they walked to the main house.

The wedding was held the following day, and the birds of all the world flew overhead, singing for joy. Rosita's father beamed with pride. The lad's mother wept once again. This time it was for happiness.

# The Silver Bell

*Denmark*

Long ago a young shepherd drove his flock of sheep into a green meadow. It was late in the afternoon, and he was tired and hungry from his day of work. He lay on the ground and, to his surprise, found a tiny silver bell in the grass.

The shepherd rang the bell and heard the sweet trill of a canary's song; or was it the sound of silver raindrops falling on a broad green leaf? Perhaps it was the sound of a mother whispering words of love to her new-born child. The most wonderful thing of all was that the shepherd no longer felt weary or hungry. His heart felt glad, and his belly felt full to bursting.

"This bell is a treasure!" he exclaimed. "I will never part with it."

The silver bell belonged to one of the dwarfs who lived under the mound at the edge of the meadow. He had been doing somersaults in the tall grass when the wee bell fell from his pocket. It was a serious matter because it was the sweet sound of the bell that put him to sleep each night. The dwarf began a careful search for his lost treasure.

Dwarfs can change their shape by whispering a magic word. First he became a squirrel in order to scamper throughout the grass. Then he became a dog and tried sniffing it out. Finally he changed into a horse in order to charge back and forth across the meadow. He had no luck. The young shepherd had taken his sheep over the low hills to another meadow quite some distance away.

The dwarf changed himself into a hawk and flew high above the hills, until at last he spied the shepherd and his flock. The hawk-dwarf circled lower and lower until he could see the bell hanging from a leather cord around the boy's neck.

The hawk landed, and the dwarf changed himself into an old woman wearing a ragged dress. She approached the shepherd saying, "My, what a pretty bell you have. Tomorrow is my granddaughter's birthday and I have no gift for her. Would you let me give her your little bell?"

"I can't give you this bell," explained the youth. "It's magical. Whenever I ring it, the world is filled with sweetness and light. My weariness melts away and my heart sings with gladness. It's the finest treasure I've ever owned."

"I see," said the old woman. "Truth be told, I'm wealthier than I appear to be. Since the bell charms me so, I'll give you this bag of gold for it." So saying, she pulled a heavy leather bag filled with gold coins from under her torn shawl.

"I'm sorry," said the boy, "but it's not for sale."

"Then listen carefully, lad, for I'm not what I seem. I'm a witch who practices magic that is white. I can give you a special staff that will bring blessings on your sheep. Your flock will increase, and you will become the wealthiest shepherd in the land."

"May I see such a staff?" asked the boy in amazement.

The old woman pulled it out from under her shawl. It was made of ivory with beautiful carvings of the biblical shepherd David playing his flute while tending his flock.

The boy felt that he could trust this

strange old woman. "Agreed!" he cried. "The silver bell for the ivory staff."

They made the exchange, and the old

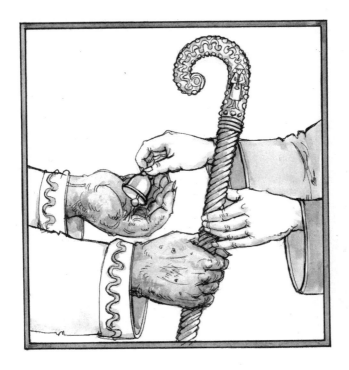

woman vanished into thin air. The surprised shepherd watched a hawk winging its way home high above him.

"Sleep," said the dwarf as he crawled into his bed that night. "At last I can sleep."

The young shepherd became a wealthy and happy man, just as the dwarf had promised.

# The Shoemaker's Dream

*Holland*

There was once a poor old shoemaker who lived in a small village, two days' walk from Amsterdam. He often dreamed of great wealth, but when he told his wife about his wonderful dreams, she laughed and said, "We can't very well eat a dream. It won't fill our empty stomachs."

One morning he awoke with a start and said, "Wife, I had a special dream last night. An angel came to me and said that I would find my fortune on the largest bridge in Amsterdam."

"Nonsense," said his sleepy wife. "Dreams are not true. You can't go off to the city when you have work here at home."

The shoemaker had the special dream again the next night. He made a decision and told his wife, "I'm going to Amsterdam to find my fortune. Nothing you can say will stop me."

It was a long and difficult journey, but at last the old man arrived in the big city. He found the largest bridge and walked across it slowly, searching for the treasure. He didn't find it. The bridge seemed quite ordinary, and the people who crossed it were just like citizens anywhere. He crossed the bridge again and again, but no treasure was found.

At last the shoemaker sat on the railing near the middle of the long expanse, waiting for something to happen. It grew dark and he sighed heavily, knowing that he would have to begin his journey home in the morning.

Just then, a ragged beggar walked up to him and said, "Please excuse my boldness, but I've noticed you looking for something on this bridge for most of the day. Perhaps I can help you find it."

"I doubt it," said the shoemaker. "A night-dream has brought me here. I'm supposed to find my fortune on this very bridge, but I don't seem to be able to locate it."

"How strange," replied the beggar. "I too have dreamed that I'd find a chest of gold. In my dream it's buried in the garden of a shoemaker who lives across the road from a small church. I don't believe in dreams, however. Everyone knows that a dream can't fill an empty stomach."

The shoemaker rushed home as fast as his legs would carry him. He had a vegetable garden behind his house, which was across the road from a small church. Ignoring his wife's many questions, he began digging up

the garden. It wasn't long before he heard
the dull thud of his hoe striking a metal
chest. He unearthed it and dragged it into
the house. The old lock, full of rust, broke

open easily. The chest was filled to the top
with golden coins!

With their fortune made, even the shoemaker's wife had to agree that sometimes
dreams can, indeed, help to fill an empty
stomach.

# Notes

The stories in this collection are my retellings of tales from throughout the world. They have come to me from written and oral sources and result from thirty years of my telling them aloud.

Seven of these tales (indicated by asterisks) were previously included in my two-volume set entitled *Pleasant Journeys: Tales to Tell from Around the World* (Mercer Island, Washington: The Writing Works, 1979), later renamed *Twenty-Two Splendid Tales to Tell From Around the World* (Little Rock: August House, 1990).

Motifs given are from *The Storyteller's Sourcebook: A Subject, Title and Motif Index to Folklore Collections for Children* by Margaret Read MacDonald (Detroit: Neal–Schuman/Gale, 1982); and *The Storyteller's Sourcebook: A Subject, Title and Motif Index to Folklore Collections for Children 1983–1999* by Margaret Read MacDonald and Brian W. Sturm (Detroit: Gale Group, 2001).

### The Book of Magic — Russia

Motif D1711.0.1.2. Based on the traditional English tale of the master and pupil wherein the apprentice calls up Beelzebub by reading the forbidden book, this Russian variant is a delight to tell. The various names of the demons were created by trial and error during many elementary school visits over the years. Have the children repeat after you, and enjoy the fun.

Other versions are found in *English Folk and Fairy Tales* by Joseph Jacobs (New York: Putman, n.d.), pp. 74–77; and *Ghosts and Spirits of Many Lands* by Freya Littledale (Garden City, New York: Doubleday, 1970), pp. 23–25.

### The Three Aunties* — Norway

Motif D2183.1. I first heard this story in 1977, in a small Seattle restaurant run by two elderly Scandinavian women. They specialized in Swedish pancakes, which one would cook and the other would serve. The Norwegian of the pair told me tales during Saturday morning breakfasts.

After telling this story, she asked, "Why do you think the other kitchen maids feared Rose's beauty?" It's a good question to ask your listeners.

A Danish variant is found in *The Golden Lynx* by Augusta Baker (Philadelphia: Lippincott, 1960), pp. 41–45.

### Red Cap and the Miser* — Ireland

Motif F236.3.2.1. My initial encounter with this fun story was during the Saint Patrick's Day Celebration in Seattle in 1981. The teller, a recent Irish immigrant, spoke with a brogue so rich that I had to ask him for clarifications after the telling. It may be more fiction than actual folktale, as I've encountered difficulty in tracing variants.

### The Shoemaker and the Elves*—Germany

Motif F381.3. My aunt gave me a picture book of this classic story for my sixth Christmas. I read and reread it many times. I love telling it still.

Other variants are found in *Household Stories* by Jakob Ludwig Karl Grimm and Wilhelm Grimm (New York: McGraw-Hill, 1886, 1966), pp. 171–172; and *The Shoemaker and the Elves* by Cynthia and William Birrer (New York: Lothrop, Lee & Shepard, 1983, pb).

### The Seven Stars*—Cherokee

Motif A773.4.1.1. The fast-moving plot and surprising and expansive ending make this a rewarding tale to tell. In the Brazilian Amazon variation, the oldest of seven brothers leads his six siblings into the sky to become the Pleiades constellation.

A Cherokee variant is found in *American Indian Tales and Legends* by Vladimir Hulpach (New York: Hamlyn, 1965), pp. 43–45.

In a Thai variant, a mother hen and her six chicks become the Pleiades. See *Thai Tales: Folk Tales of Thailand* by Supaporn Vathanaprida (Englewood, Colorado: Libraries Unlimited, 1994), pp. 39–41.

### The Old Man with a Wart*—Japan

Motif F344.1.1. This is an excellent tale for classroom enactment. You play the narrator and select two boys or girls for the old folks' roles. Everyone else plays the Storm Spirits. Trust the children to create an entertaining dance.

I first discovered this story in *Fairy Tales of the Orient* by Pearl S. Buck (New York: Simon & Schuster, 1965), pp. 232–236. A German variant is found in *The Complete Fairy Tales of the Brothers Grimm* by Jack Zipes (New York: Bantam Books, 1992), pp. 576–578.

### The Birds of All the World—Spain

Motif D431.1. Enchantment and transformation are core to magic of all kinds. This popular Spanish tale is a variant of the German tale of transformation from carnation to person. I discovered it in *Tales of Enchantment from Spain* by Elsie Spicer Eells (New York: Dodd-Mead, 1950), pp. 15–24. See also *Grimms' Fairy Tales* by Jakob Ludwig Karl Grimm and Wilhelm Grimm (New York: World, 1947), pp. 93–98.

### The Silver Bell* — Denmark

Motif P451.5.1.5.0.3. As a general rule in the realms of enchantment, dwarfs tend to be much more generous than leprechauns and trolls. The dwarf's transformations to hawk and old woman will delight your listeners.

I discovered this tale in *A Book of Dwarfs* by Ruth Manning-Sanders (New York: Dutton, 1963), pp. 89–94. An interesting variant is found in *Celebrate the World: Twenty Tellable Folktales for Multicultural Festivals* by Margaret Read MacDonald (New York: H.W. Wilson, 1994), pp. 184–192.

### The Shoemaker's Dream* — Holland

Motif N531.1. With the proliferation of state lotteries, I often ask my listeners if they have dreamed of winning big. "What if," I then ask, "you dreamed of four of the six numbers? How would you obtain the other two?" Then I tell this tale.

Variants are found in *Tricky Peik and Other Picture Tales* by Jeanne B. Hardendorff (Philadelphia: Lippincott, 1967), pp. 33–39; and *The Priceless Cats and Other Italian Folk Stories* by Moritz A. Jagendorf (New York: Vanguard, 1956), pp. 35–39.